Between Worlds

REALITY AMIDST THE TRUTH

BY

RAMONA

131 Finsbury Pavement, London EC2A 1NT

https://www.theempirepublishers.co.uk/

Our books may be purchased in bulk for promotional, educational, or business use.

Please contact The Empire Publishers at +44 20 4579 8116, or by email at support@theempirepublishers.co.uk

First Edition December 2024

About the Author

Spirituality and magic have captivated Ramona from a young age. Her work seamlessly blends real-life events with vivid imagination, bringing together the tangible and the mystical. Fascinated by the unknown, Ramona's lifelong quest for understanding drives her storytelling.

Drawing from her personal experiences, Ramona offers a unique spiritual perspective on life. She believes that while nothing in this world is permanent, our souls are eternal. Her writing explores this profound truth, inviting readers to contemplate the deeper aspects of existence.

Ramona's journey into the unknown has been transformative, and she seeks to share this life-changing connection with her readers.

Her work is a testament to her belief that spirituality and magic can profoundly impact our lives, offering insights and inspiration that resonate on a soul-deep level.

Dedication

I want to dedicate this book to Andreea Ştan. I had the idea of writing a book for a long time but never knew where to start, so I gave up. I just wrote for myself, thinking it was an impossible dream. Then, on a random day, while searching the internet, I met Andreea. From the first moment I spoke with her, I knew this was the path I would take.

She provided all the details about publishing a book and kept in touch with me for almost a year before I started this project. Andreea has always been friendly and supportive, being there whenever I needed an answer or any information.

Andreea gave me hope that this book could exist in the real world, not just in my imagination. I dedicate this book to her because, without her, it would never have become a reality.

Thank you, Andreea!

Acknowledgements

I want to thank you, Michelle Adam, my project manager, for being so supportive and nurturing with my book. I appreciate your patience in bringing my ideas to fruition and sharing my excitement for this project.

I also want to thank you, Dianne Williams, my editor, who brought so much hard work and, with my creativity and her skills, created a new way of writing a book, from one idea to thousands of ideas, bringing it all together in this unique publication.

Thank you, The Empire Publishers, for bringing a dream into reality!

Table of Contents

Childhood

Childhood

Ramy, a scrawny little girl with big brown eyes was born in the poverty-stricken village in the heart of Romania, Cucuiata Din Deal. It bordered a lush forest, where no human civilisation dared to prevail. Only animals; bears, boars, reindeer, rabbits, and other creatures hidden in the darkness of the damp woods thrived.

The girl, a child to poor parents and a threat to a mean old granny residing in their humble abode, was one with nature.

The brown in her eyes mirrored the majestic aura of the forest that scared the biggest of hearts, but she was not born to be a coward. That was one thing fate had clearly sorted out for her.

Ramy was born special.

It was in the way she would sway her head and close her eyes at the sound of any music, the way her little body enveloped with an electric buzz, that if you'd touch her skin, you'd feel a current go through you.

It was in the way she looked at you.

It was in the way her eyes would twinkle when an animal would find its way to her backyard, looking for food, and how she would run back in the kitchen, fetch the leftover food, even at the cost of receiving punishment from her granny, and feed the deranged creature with a knowing smile spread on her face.

It was in the way her mother knew that when there were days her heart couldn't take the harshness of the world, she could just have a look at her daughter and every single pain of hers would vanish as if it never existed in the first place.

When the tired greyness of her mother's eyes met the soft brown of her daughter's, all the pain evaporated in the musky air around them, and the only thing she would feel was love.

But this was in all the good ways that Ramy felt different. There was a side, that she had hidden from everyone.

A side she wanted to keep away from the eyes of the world, from her own being as well, but only if she could.

She was only a child then, after all.

That side would find her tucked under her blanket, her hands blocking her ears to the heaving of her mother outside, as she would scrub and clean the chipped flooring, getting it to shine, as per the instructions of no one else but her granny. "I want the floor to shine like a silver nickel, you hear me, woman?!" The way her heart would thunder with rage, and her hands would shiver with restraint.

Some nights, she would feel her anger boiling into the pit of her stomach, and dread would creep into her little heart.

The rocky, chipped wooden cot would vibrate under her, and heat would dissipate from every single cell in her body.

Those nights, when she would finally be able to sleep, she would dream of black crows and fire. A house engulfed in a destructive orange hue, while a flock of black crows encircle the charred roof. She would wake up, sweaty and trembling.

During one such night, she woke up in the morning with a blinding ache in her head.

Her entire body felt like it was thrown against a wall, as it hurt with every slight movement.

When she walked out of her room to fetch some water, she found her granny, her washed-out grey locks secured in a braid, which was swaying right and left, as she filled her mouth with freshly baked bread, the special breakfast that Ramy's mother had cooked for her mother-in-law but couldn't eat herself, as she was already mowing the lawn outside under the scorching sun.

Ramy's core burned with anger, and her eyes narrowed at the old wicked woman, who had never left any chance to wound her mother and herself.

She could only dream of having a normal day in this house where she would wake up not dreading the abuses all ready to be showered upon her by her grandmother. The most difficult part was the attitude of the old woman that made them suffer the most with no power against her, just to execute the order of being captured, with no rights or anything they could do against her.

Michaella was a woman of force, but the air around her always reeked of envy, hatred, and angst for the world.

That woman seemed to only breathe negativity.

But it was something else when it was directed towards her granddaughter and the woman who gave birth to her.

Ramy's mother, Maya, was one innocent soul. She was born in a meagre family, to a mother who was murdered in cold blood at the hands of her very own husband.

The man was nothing short of a devil's spawn, always furious and taking the wrath of his failures on his angel-like wife. Every brunt of his fall was felt the most by his wife, and she never uttered a word. She took it all without a complaint slipping out from her mouth.

When she was thirty-seven years old, her husband's uncontrolled fury ended her life. Unfortunately, life had not given up on testing Maya, as she was married off to a man, whose tongue was bound to silence in front of his malicious mother's evil doings.

It was as if he was under a spell, where he was blind, deaf, and dumb whenever his mother would inflict the worst kind of pain on the woman whom he was supposed to protect. To love. To care for.

Maya felt the shackles of misery around her neck and limbs loosen up when she heard news of her pregnancy.

She prayed and prayed and prayed. But if you would see her while praying – her eyes pinched close, her cheeks stained with moisture, and her hands clasped together, her body rocking back and forth, it would look like she was begging; pleading with God to show all the mercy that He didn't bestow upon her to her child. She wanted nothing but her child to be an excuse for her to continue living.

To come out of the misery that had plagued her life. In her mind, her child had to be a reason for her to start looking forward in life.

When she first laid her eyes on a palm-sized baby, her almond, brown eyes shimmering with curiosity as they inspected the woman who just pushed her out of her womb, she felt seen. All the love in the world blossomed in her with such force that it almost choked her. She whispered, "my Ramy..." Her baby, all warm and cosy in her arms, smiled wide upon hearing such a comforting sound.

Experiencing that, Maya herself was welcomed into the most delighted slumber, something that she had never experienced before.

Maybe it was the realisation that God had finally heard her prayers, that she had Him on her side after all this time. She was not alone anymore.

As Ramy grew up, Michaella's fury only seemed to increase tenfold, and the receiving end did not just point towards Maya. Ramy was also an equal recipient now.

Michaella would find immense pleasure in keeping the mother and the daughter suffering. She would deprive them of rest, make them work worse than the barnyard donkeys, and make them feel useless in front of her.

As the flashbacks of her granny hurling abuses at her and her mother day and night as they wasted away their bodies stormed into her mind, causing something to stir inside her. She didn't know if it was because of the way her body was hurting, or it was the anger punching her heart, but Ramy felt this strong urge to close her eyes, and as she did, her arms outstretched from her body, reaching the back of her granny's wrinkled neck.

She felt both her hands snake around her grooved skin.

A wave of ire infiltrated her veins, and she pressed her fingers hard around her throat. Michaella's blood gurgled and thumped under the little girl's touch.

A strange melody reached Ramy's ears.

Just when the notes seemed to intensify, Ramy heard her granny coughing, and scoffing, fighting for some air, her ragged hands thrashing against hers. Just when her granny's hands started to loosen their grip, and her breathing became more and more haggard, Ramy opened her eyes.

She found herself standing where she was.

But her hands, instead of choking the woman she despised from the bottom of her heart, were by her side, in a fist. The only sound of breathing falling on her ears was hers – frantic and dishevelled.

Her granny turned around, a curious look on her ancient face. Not uttering a single word, she walked out and disappeared into the garden.

Ramy, trembling with dread, came inside her room and sat in front of the shabby mirror adorning the wall opposite her bed. She met her brown eyes through her reflection, fear brimming in them.

Michaella barked from the garden, "Wake up, Ramy, you good-for-nothing bastard. There is a pile of clothes and dishes to be washed!"

That morning, Ramy knew she could be dangerous.

That morning, she knew she had to protect her loved ones, not just from the evils of the outside world, but also from the demon that she felt resided inside her. Ramy was only seven years old when she vowed to herself, on a random, October morning, that she would never let the anger inside her take control over her. She was terrified of the thought alone.

After that incident, she tried to be as normal as she could be, she closed off and tried to pretend to be good and friendly with other children. Ramy reduced herself to being ordinary; being scared of herself and when she was picked on by bullies, she knew that this was happening because she was different. When she would enter the house, bruised and bloody, after being beaten up by bigger kids, her granny would demand her presence in the garden. She was full of anger, but she didn't dare to protest. With the little energy left, she would take care of her gardening chores, and then go to her room to get cleaned.

Maya would bring in whatever Michaella had left for them to munch on for her daughter after they were done with the chores, and Ramy would eat with a gentle smile on her face. At least she had her mother by her side, that was the only reassurance that brought some relief to her hurting heart.

On a good day, when Michaella would be under the weather and lock herself in the room, Maya would cover for her daughter, and she'd go out and play in the forest, a little music player clutched in her hand. She would sit under a tree, near a pond, and listen to the music.

It was only a melody, no words. But it seemed to Ramy that the music notes were able to converse with her. They would whisper words of love and belonging, telling her that she is not alone and that she belongs here, with them.

Nature and music seemed to bring her alive, and open her mind to everything that was awake around her. Every element of the mucky Earth under her, the humid air surrounding her, and the blue water in the pond moving softly against the soil bed, appeared to understand her, know her.

She felt the most seen here, or maybe, it was she who could see everything when she was here, as she was accompanied by gentle notes and the embrace of the universe.

***

Ramy had been a target of dark forces from the very moment she entered this world. The evil powers wanted her dead, believing that if she survived, her strength would be too much for this realm to contain.

But the poor child, so innocent, had no idea that her life was already condemned—destined to be one of hardship, with little hope of experiencing what most would call a "normal" life.

The struggles she faced were not of her own making, yet she would bear them.

But who will triumph in the end? The evil that seeks to destroy her, or the special creature who defies fate at every turn? Nobody could tell, but only time.

At just three years old, one of these moments unfolded. Eager to find her mother, Ramy called out to her, wandering into the garden. When no response came, a pang of loneliness swept over her, and tears welled in her eyes. Then she heard it—her mother's voice, faint, calling from the basement. With the innocence of a child, Ramy rushed toward the voice, not knowing the danger that awaited her.

The staircase was steep, and as her small feet misjudged the narrow steps, she tumbled, rolling violently down until she hit the cold ground.

Maya, her mother, was terrified when she found Ramy—her tiny body bloodied and breathless at the foot of the stairs. Screaming for help, Maya gently washed her daughter and called an ambulance. Guilt consumed her, as she wept for what had happened to her child. Ramy slipped into a coma. While Maya was devastated, her grandmother secretly rejoiced, hoping this would finally end the life of the "creature" she despised so deeply.

Yet, outwardly, she wore the mask of concern, pretending to care. Little did she know that Ramy's spirit was far stronger than her frail body.

Ramy miraculously recovered, but not without further complications. A doctor mistakenly administered an extra dose of medication, causing her heart to race uncontrollably, plunging her back into unconsciousness.

Her family braced for the worst, certain that this would be the end. The air was thick with the grim weight of preparing for a funeral.

Yet against all odds, after three months, Ramy survived. All that remained of the traumatic incident was a faint scar near her left eyebrow—a constant, aching reminder of her near-death experience. Her recovery shocked even the doctors, as no one expected such a fragile child to endure so much. Clearly, a higher power had plans for her, despite the evil forces that sought to claim her.

Years passed, but the danger never left. When she was twelve, another close call nearly took her life. While crossing the street, a speeding car appeared out of nowhere, missing her by just a few centimeters. Frozen in fear, Ramy ran home in tears, her heart pounding with terror. Her mother, seeing her

daughter's distress, comforted her, gently reminding her to thank God for her narrow escape.

With a weak smile, Maya tried to lighten the mood, comparing Ramy to a cat with nine lives.

But deep inside, Maya knew the truth: her daughter was a beacon, attracting both light and darkness. She was a target for evil, and though Maya prayed fervently, she knew the battle would be long. Ramy's journey was far from over, and only time would tell whether her life would continue to be overshadowed by dark clouds or if, one day, she would emerge into the light.

Adolescence

Adolescence

Ramy's journey through life felt like navigating a colourless landscape, where every day blended into the next in a dull rhythm. Lost in the shadows of her existence, she couldn't see beyond the monotony.

But then, on an ordinary day, a chance encounter changed everything. Ramy's friend, Rea, introduced her to Michael.

That day seemed no different from any other, as she walked across the old stone bridge with Rea, her friend who had accompanied her home from college countless times before. The bridge was a familiar path, and her mind drifted in and out of conversation, lulled by the sound of their footsteps. But then, amid the usual chatter, Rea stopped suddenly, her face lighting up as she waved to someone in the distance. The unexpected gesture broke Ramy's trance.

"Ramy, this is Michael," Rea said, her voice carrying an excitement Ramy hadn't heard in a while.

As Ramy's eyes met his, something shifted. There was nothing particularly remarkable about the introduction, yet in that moment, time seemed to slow. The steady rhythm of her life had found a beat, a subtle, new cadence that hinted at a change she hadn't realised she was waiting for.

After that first meeting on the bridge, their paths crossed more frequently. It was as if fate had quietly woven Michael into Ramy's daily routine. As she walked to college each morning, she would often spot him waiting nearby, casually leaning against the railing, his eyes lighting up as soon as she approached.

There was a relaxed confidence about him, an ease that came from the freedom his private school schedule afforded him. Michael didn't have to be anywhere at any specific time—he could choose his own hours, his own path, leaving him with plenty of time to explore whatever, or whoever, piqued his interest.

For him, that first encounter on the bridge had been enough. Something about Ramy had captured his attention, a quiet intrigue that drew him in. She was different—he couldn't quite put his finger on why, but he wanted to know more.

The casual conversations they had after class became a ritual he looked forward to, moments that broke up the structureless nature of his days.

While Ramy walked her familiar route to and from college, Michael was there, always waiting, as if he had known exactly where to find her.

It was easy for him—her commute was predictable, and so was her presence. But what wasn't predictable, at least for Ramy, was the way those conversations slowly started to affect her. At first, it felt like a simple companionship, someone to talk to.

Yet, the more they spoke, the more she began to notice how effortlessly their words flowed, how Michael had a way of making the most ordinary topics feel fascinating.

Each day, their exchanges grew longer. Michael, with his free-spirited schedule, would accompany her part of the way home, talking about everything and nothing at once. Ramy found herself intrigued by his spontaneity, the way his life seemed to unfold without the rigid structure that defined her own. There was something refreshing in his ability to do what he wanted, whenever he pleased. For him, time was abundant, and he seemed content to spend it discovering more about her.

Unbeknownst to Ramy, Michael had already decided that she was someone he wanted to keep close. He didn't need a schedule or plan to see her—he only needed to follow the familiar rhythm of her daily life, knowing she would be there, day after day. And as their conversations deepened, so too did his feelings.

At first, Ramy felt distant, her heart shielded from any new connections. Yet, Michael saw beyond her walls. He found her captivating, her mysterious aura drawing him in. Intrigued, he sought to unravel the layers of her story from afar, eager to discover more about her.

Michael, with his wit and understanding, created a haven where Ramy felt secure. As their friendship blossomed, they began to realise that their bond ran deeper than mere companionship. Slowly but surely, their feelings for each other grew, and Ramy experienced a sensation she had never known before: Love.

In each other's presence, they found solace, their connection electric and profound. With Michael, Ramy finally understood what it meant to be truly seen and understood. Their love was intense, a flame that illuminated the darkness of their pasts.

However, despite their deep connection, they had to keep their love hidden because Ramy's grandmother would never approve. They were like puzzle pieces that fit perfectly together, but they couldn't show it to the world.

But Ramy could sense her granny's health deteriorating with each passing day. With that, the strong hold of Michaela on her granddaughter was also loosening up, which offered Ramy some peace in her life, and she carried on with her secret love life like nothing monumental was happening.

Ramy found solace and grounding in the presence of Michael, who brought a sense of reality to her world. Yet, one fateful night, as she lost herself in the melody of music before drifting off to sleep, she encountered a mysterious figure delivering a message: her grandmother's impending demise. Despite the clarity of the message, Ramy brushed it off as nothing more than a dream.

As time passed, her grandmother's health deteriorated rapidly, until one morning, she passed away.

Ramy was overcome with a profound sense of foreboding, realising that her earlier intuition had been a premonition of the impending tragedy. However, she failed to heed her own intuition and predictions, choosing instead to dismiss them as mere fleeting thoughts.

After Michaela's death, Ramy thought that fate would give her a breather – some time to heal and relish in freedom, but she was unaware of one thing – fate had other ideas pre-planned and all ready to unravel for her, only at a time when she wasn't expecting anything at the least.

After finishing school, Ramy and Michael faced the challenge of finding jobs. It was harder for Michael because he didn't have a degree that could help him find a sustainable job.

When Michael got an offer to move abroad, Ramy had a big decision to make. After talking it over and thinking things through, she chose to join him on this new adventure.

But things didn't go as planned. They ended up in a tough situation, working without proper papers and living with people who took advantage of them.

They were treated badly and worked too much, like they were stuck in a prison without bars – slaving away their days in a dirty kitchen, just to be paid in cash under the table.

Despite their struggles, they held onto hope and tried to find a way out of their difficult circumstances. But it wasn't easy. They were young and didn't fully understand the dangers they were facing. All they could do was cling to each other and dream of a better future.

The Escape

The Escape

In the midst of uncertainty, they grappled with the weight of their options, torn between returning to their homeland or seeking an alternative path. It was then that Ramy's spirit of adventure ignited, breathing life into Michael with the prospect of escape and navigating their predicament with cunning strategy.

In the depths of their hardship, they found themselves compelled to hold secret discussions outside their dwelling, speaking in hushed tones to evade any hint of

suspicion. Mapping out their escape became their sole mission, necessitating silent walks and covert exchanges, miles away from prying eyes, before they could dare to breathe freely and communicate without fear.

They met in a park far from their home, a few streets away, hiding in the shadows of an abandoned, dilapidated house.

The crumbling walls and overgrown weeds made it the perfect cover, a place where no one would think to look for them. Here, they laid their plans, pouring over every detail, every risk, and every fleeting opportunity.

Their first hurdle was finding a place to live. They whispered of agencies and landlords, debating whether to trust strangers or take their chances asking around the neighbourhood. Ramy suggested they look for anyone willing to rent out a spare room, but even that came with complications. Trust was scarce in these uncertain times, and each day they went without a stable home was another day filled with danger.

"We need to make a plan," Ramy said, her voice barely a whisper. "We can't just wait and hope something falls into our laps. We have to be strategic."

Michael nodded, scribbling numbers in a small, worn notebook. They sketched out a budget, calculating how much they needed to save, and how far their meagre earnings would take them. Rent, food, transportation—everything was accounted for, but the numbers still didn't add up.

"Even if we find a room, we need working documents," Michael added, his brow furrowed. "Without them, we can't open a bank account, we can't legally work, and we'll be stuck in this limbo forever."

Their talks grew more intense as they considered the bureaucracy they would have to navigate.

Applications for residency, work permits, bank accounts—each step felt like scaling a mountain, and the fear of failure weighed heavily on them both. They made lists of contacts, agencies they could approach, and the paperwork they needed to gather. The possibility of being turned away or denied lingered in the air, but they had no choice but to press on.

"What if we can't find a proper job?" Michael asked, the doubt creeping into his voice. "What if it takes months? We don't have the luxury of time."

"We'll need a backup plan," Ramy replied, her gaze steady.

"We have to find a way to stretch our money. If that means doing odd jobs, so be it. We just need enough to stay afloat until something better comes along. In the worst-case scenario, we go back to Romania, but at least we are trying our best." She looked at an anxious Michael, hoping her words would calm his nerves.

Their escape plan became a series of contingencies—what to do if they ran out of money, where to turn if their documents were delayed, how long they could hold out before having to make the impossible decision to leave.

Every possibility was accounted for, from the worst-case scenario to the faintest glimmer of hope.

By the time they parted ways, the sun had begun to set, casting long shadows over their hidden meeting spot. The weight of their mission was clear, but so too was their determination.

Together, they would navigate the labyrinth of their new world, even if it meant taking risks that could cost them everything.

Luckily, Michael found someone who knew of rooms for rent, they were fortunate to speak English, which helped them navigate their plans.

They kept their escape plan secret, with Ramy meticulously calculating every detail to avoid suspicion.

She was used to keeping her head low, as she had a childhood where she was always walking on eggshells. The hard part was finding a place to live that would help keep their heads above water and work in a reputable place all at the same time.

Eventually, they secured a room and gathered enough money to sustain themselves until they found better opportunities.

Moving their belongings without raising suspicion was a challenge, but they managed it with the help of an individual – a friend who was working with a company that helped bring people in and out to different countries; however, what he was being used for in this case was his valuable information and the fact that he owned a car. Finally, one morning, they made their move. With keys to their new home in hand, they waited for their boss to leave before contacting their ride. They carefully hid their belongings and acted as inconspicuously as possible. Ramy supported Michael through his nerves, and together they successfully relocated to their new home without a trace.

Their former managers were furious when they realized Ramy and Michael were gone after they went to hunt them down as they were not responding to their messages, but their escape was flawless. They were now free to work legally and had a place to stay.

However, their troubles were far from over. In their new shared house, they encountered an alcoholic tenant who developed an irrational hatred for Michael. For no reason, he would make Michael a target and rile him up with provoking slurs.

One day, the same guy, nobody knew his name, pulled out a knife and threatened Michael, telling him that he would cut him in pieces if he ever touched things in the kitchen. Just because Michael moved a plate that belonged to the person on the counter one morning, the man who was silently observing him from behind pounced on him, and threatened Michael with murder. There was a thing about Michael's behaviour that pushed this mentally deranged individual to the edge.

Despite reporting the incident to the landlord, they received no help and decided to move again, as Michael was not ready to compromise on their safety.

Room 6

Room 6

For a while, they found peace, but three years later, tragedy struck. She had finally started to live a normal life, forgetting about her tragic childhood, the unsettling energies that she would often feel around her, and the negativities that had been following her around like a hungry wolf, but as fate had it, she was still to come across something that threatened to change the entire course of her life, and only for the bad.

After Ramy and Michael came back from a much needed vacation, Ramy lost her job. Her work place closed down for good, and left her without an income. However, whenever bad news knocked on her door, it never came alone, but brought with itself a world of darkness.

Around the same time, Ramy started feeling strange things in the house. At first, she brushed it off, thinking it was just in her head, a byproduct of stress and exhaustion.

But as the nights dragged on, the unease deepened. It began with unsettling dreams—nightmares that clung to her mind even after waking. One night, she felt an unseen hand tugging at her blanket, as if someone or something was trying to pull it away. The sensation was too real, too vivid to be a dream, and it left her paralyzed with fear.

Night after night, the strange occurrences continued, intensifying with each passing day. Ramy noticed odd things: shadows flickering in her peripheral vision, the sound of footsteps in empty hallways, and whispers she couldn't quite catch.

She convinced herself it was just the creaks of an old building, or her imagination running wild, but deep down, she couldn't shake the feeling that something was wrong. Someone—or something—was watching her.

Then there were the nights when Michael wasn't home. Those were the worst. Alone in the house, she became hyper-aware of every creak and shift in the air. Shadows seemed darker, and every small sound felt like a warning. The sense of being observed grew unbearable, even though she was the only one there. Or so it seemed.

One evening, as she walked through the dimly lit corridor, her eyes were drawn to room 6. She realized she hadn't seen the tenant who lived there in quite some time.

At first, she thought nothing of it. People came and went. But as she checked in with the other residents, a gnawing suspicion grew. No one had seen him. Days turned into weeks, and the absence became more pronounced, gnawing at her mind like a dark omen.

Her anxiety built to a crescendo the night the phone began to ring.

The shrill, insistent sound echoed through the empty corridor, sending shivers down her spine. No one was around to answer it, but the ringing continued. As it did, Ramy's anxiety surged, her thoughts racing toward grim possibilities. What if something had happened to the tenant of room 6? Her gut screamed at her that something was terribly wrong.

"Michael," she whispered, her voice trembling. "I think something's happened. I haven't seen him in weeks. I..." Her eyes looked bewildered, and she gulped heavily after saying the words, which wreaked havoc in her mind.

"I think he is dead or...or something very bad has happened to him, Michael."

Michael, however, seemed unfazed by her concerns, offering a dismissive laugh. "Why would he be dead in his room? That doesn't make any sense," he reasoned, attempting to lighten the mood.

But Ramy couldn't shake the feeling. She insisted, and with an exaggerated sigh, Michael finally agreed to check it out. He knocked on the door of room 6. No response. The phone was still ringing inside. The knot in Ramy's stomach tightened. Michael hesitated before slowly pushing the door open.

The stench hit him first, a wave of rotting air that made him recoil. Ramy saw his face go pale, his eyes wide with shock. "He's... he's dead," Michael stammered, stumbling back into the hallway.

Ramy's heart plummeted. It was real. The fear that had been clawing at her mind for weeks now had a horrifying reality. They called the police, and the investigation that followed was swift and procedural. But for Ramy, the nightmare was just beginning.

Over the next few months, her nights were plagued by nightmares and unsettling disturbances.

Scratching sounds at her door and window, faint voices that seemed to call her name, the thud of something heavy hitting the floor when no one was around. She found dead birds on her windowsill, their lifeless bodies a grotesque offering she didn't understand. The presence of something sinister enveloped the house, but no one else seemed to feel it the way she did.

Ramy was no stranger to fear, but this was different. She sensed something was following her, clinging to her every step. It wasn't just the house; it was something deeper, something reaching out to her from beyond.

The ghost of the man from room 6 hadn't moved on, and Ramy had unknowingly become his anchor.

The more time passed, the more trapped she felt. The house became her prison, a place where the boundary between the living and the dead blurred. Each night, she felt the presence closer, lurking at the edge of her consciousness. Sometimes, she would wake up in the middle of the night, drenched in cold sweat, certain she wasn't alone in her room. The sensation of something wrapping around her, like a snake, tightening with each breath, left her frozen in terror.

For eight long months, Ramy remained locked in this cycle of fear, haunted by a presence that no one else could feel. Michael, ever the skeptic, couldn't understand why she was so affected. He couldn't see what she saw, couldn't hear the whispers that tormented her.

As time wore on, Ramy's fear turned inward. She couldn't live like this forever. Her job situation worsened as she was made redundant, and the stress of being trapped in the house amplified her despair.

Desperate for answers, she began to research everything she could about spirits, the afterlife, and the connection between worlds. She sought understanding, turning to spiritual texts and psychological studies, hoping to find a way to make sense of her experiences.

In her search, she discovered something unexpected: the power she held. Ramy wasn't just a victim of the haunting—she was a conduit. The ghost of the man from room 6 had chosen her because she was the only one who could help him. He was trapped between worlds, unable to move on, and Ramy had the ability to bridge that gap.

At first, she resisted the idea. Why her? Why was she the one chosen to bear this burden? She wasn't ready. But as the disturbances grew more intense, she realized she had no choice. The spirit wasn't going to leave until she helped him. Ramy's journey into the unknown began as she tapped into her newfound connection to the spiritual realm.

This wasn't just a haunting—it was an awakening. Ramy could feel the threads of energy that connected the world of the living to the realm of the spirits, and she was learning to navigate them.

What had once seemed like a curse was slowly becoming a power, a gift that allowed her to bring knowledge from the other world into this one.

But with this gift came responsibility. The spirit from room 6 was not the only one who would seek her out. Ramy was opening a door to the 4th dimension, a higher plane of existence where spirits lingered, waiting for closure, for help, for peace. Her transformation was just beginning, and the journey ahead would be unlike anything she had ever imagined. Her life, once tethered to the mundane, was now intertwined with the supernatural. And there was no turning back.

From the shadows of an unseen realm, Ramy's every step, every sigh, every tear, was witnessed by eyes that saw beyond the veil of reality. In a dimension unfathomable to mortal minds, the Unseen watched, their existence a whispered secret in the fabric of the universe.

"Poor creature," one murmured, their voice laden with sorrow, as they beheld Ramy's trials. "She doesn't know what is waiting for her."

In the ethereal expanse, where time danced to a different rhythm and space was but a fleeting concept, voices mingled in a symphony of concern.

"It's just the beginning of her suffering," another voice lamented, their words echoing in the void. Spheres of light encircled Ramy, their glow tinged with a melancholy hue, as if mourning the hardships yet to come.

"She is not going to make it," a somber tone asserted, casting a shadow over the unseen audience. "It is too much for her."

But amidst the chorus of doubt and despair, there arose a lone voice, defiant in its optimism, a beacon of hope amidst the encroaching darkness.

"She needs to pass the test!" it proclaimed, its words resounding with unwavering conviction.

And Ramy, unaware of the unseen eyes that observed her every struggle, pressed on, driven by a flicker of determination that burned within her soul. She clung to the belief that every trial must have an end, every storm must eventually subside. Yet little did she know, that for her, the journey was far from over.

In her world, where the mundane met the extraordinary, where the line between reality and illusion blurred, Ramy fought for survival with a courage born of desperation.

But as she dared to dream of a semblance of normalcy, life, in its cruel irony, conspired to remind her that for her, there would be no respite.

"Not for you, Ramy," whispered the unseen chorus, their voices a haunting refrain in the vast expanse of the unknown. "Not for you, special creature."

And so, Ramy walked the tightrope between despair and hope, her path illuminated by the unseen gaze of those who watched from realms beyond. Unaware of the unseen forces that guided her fate, she pressed onward, a solitary figure in a world teetering on the brink of chaos, her heart heavy with the weight of the unseen burdens that lay ahead.

***

Michael's behaviour toward Ramy changed, marking a significant shift in their relationship. He found a new job opportunity that paid much more, but it required them to move to a different location.

After eight months, they relocated to a big city with more opportunities, hoping to leave their troubles behind. Ramy found a new job, and they began saving money to furnish their ideal home.

Over time, they began to argue. Michael wanted Ramy to work with him, but she resisted, feeling that a career in engineering wasn't right for her. He couldn't understand her perspective and became more possessive and controlling. This transformation marked a new chapter in their relationship.

Past Lives

Past Lives

From a young age, Ramy possessed a unique gift. She could pick up information from sounds and transform them into vivid visions from other dimensions. Through meditation, she tapped into different frequencies, allowing her mind to traverse realms and unravel the mysteries of time and existence.

In her mind's eye, Ramy witnessed snippets of lives — some from the past, others from realms unknown.

Each vision unveiled a tale woven with threads of different people, backgrounds, and times. Among the myriad visions, a few stood out with remarkable clarity.

One such vision transported Ramy to a sunny garden, where two children, a boy and a girl aged four, giggled and played. Their laughter filled the air, but a grumpy neighbour's voice shattered the joyous moment. "Don't laugh! Stop laughing! It's irritating!" he scolded. Undeterred, the children sought refuge in the basement, finding solace in their game with a ball.

Yet, in another glimpse, the same children appeared in a grayscale world, tears streaming down their faces in a desolate cemetery. They mourned the loss of their mother before meeting a tragic end together at yet another time. Across various parallel lives, it seemed their bond endured, transcending the barriers of time and circumstance.

Another vision plunged Ramy into the heart of medieval romance and tragedy. She saw a noble lady and a humble horseman deeply in love, their relationship condemned by the rigid societal norms of their time.

The brutal intervention of knights tore them apart, leading to the horseman's death and the lady's imprisonment in a dark tunnel. The horseman's dying declaration of eternal love, and his vow to reunite with her in another life, resonated deeply within Ramy, highlighting themes of love, sacrifice, and the quest for reunion beyond the grave.

However, a more frequent vision that had been haunting Ramy since she was a child was of a burning house. It was owned by Black Crow.

He was an agent who, instead of protecting the sanctity of his country, was violating the law of securing government information and giving it away to the enemies for the benefit of a more luxurious life.

Ramy saw herself as an official spy in this vision, known as Black Eyes, a diligent, vigilant loyalist to his country, who caught Black Crow red-handed, and as punishment, the traitor's house was flattened with a raging fire – purely directed by the government. Black Eyes was a man of word, and ethics, but he was deeply engrossed in his own world of bringing justice.

He was always seen covered, no feature of his for display, not even his eyes, hence, the name Black Eyes was what became of his identity.

As for the vision, it would always conclude with a pair of eyes reflecting fire, the cruelness in them was something that reminded Ramy of her grandmother. Later, she would find out that it was, indeed, the Black Crow who had embodied Michaela in this life, and her painful death as Black Crow embedded in her memory from her past life was the cause of all the injustice thrown at Ramy's way when she was a child.

Her strong feelings, combined with different sounds, transported Ramy into worlds that seemed impossible for ordinary people to understand or imagine, especially for Michael. For a long time, Ramy didn't know she had this special power. She went through life without understanding the mysteries hidden within her own thoughts. It wasn't until she faced problems in her relationship with Michael that she began to realize something strange was happening.

As her relationship with Michael grew increasingly strained, Ramy's awareness of her unique ability sharpened.

The music that once served as mere background noise now seemed to whisper secrets of alternate worlds, urging her to delve deeper into the enigmatic visions. In the solitude of her introspective moments, she pondered the significance of these experiences, gradually uncovering layers of her hidden power.

After a while, Ramy found refuge in this world, finding herself captured between worlds. The world of her imagination became more exciting for her, and she began to neglect her real world, with Michael being the first victim.

Michael wasn't strong enough to pull Ramy back into reality, so Ramy found solace in the other world, waking up just for survival, work, and food.

In another vision, a black-and-white scene unfolded, revealing a five-year-old girl who loved cats. Unfortunately, she had a neighbour who was a cat killer. Whenever this man saw a cat, it was as if he saw the Devil in front of him. He took her cat, put it in a bag, and after three days, he threw the cat to his hungry dogs, giving the girl cookies instead of her beloved pet, feeding on her tears.

This little girl's suffering etched itself into the history of her soul. In a parallel life, the same girl appeared as a queen, caring for the palace's cats.

The cat killer was now in prison, left without food and water, dying because he had tried to kill the queen and her cats out of jealousy of her kindness and beauty.

As Ramy's life increasingly revolved around her visions, her real-world interactions dwindled. Her life transformed into something she had once thought impossible, yet the impossible became reality for this special creature. Sometimes, one might wonder if she was real or mystical.

The escalating difficulties with Michael acted as a catalyst, intensifying Ramy's connection to the mysterious visions. She felt an irresistible pull towards these alternate realities, as if they were not merely figments of her imagination but beckoning beacons from a realm that felt strangely like home. This universe, though bizarre and unfamiliar, began to resonate with her, offering a sense of belonging and purpose that contrasted starkly with the chaos of her current life.

Ramy's journey into the depths of her own mind and the alternate dimensions it revealed became an exploration of self-discovery and empowerment.

Each vision provided clues to the interconnectedness of existence, urging her to embrace her gift and the profound insights it offered.

As she navigated the complexities of her relationship with Michael and the compelling allure of her visions, Ramy embarked on a transformative quest to understand her place in the vast, intricate web of life that spanned across dimensions and lifetimes.

In Another
World

In Another World

In another world, trees aren't just trees. They possess a consciousness of their own, communicating silently with each other. They bear witness to the pain and suffering of all creatures on the planet, striving to cleanse the world of negativity. Though they hold countless stories within their silent depths, the trees remain steadfast in their duty, preserving knowledge within their frequencies.

Within the dystopian confines of the forest in this world, a secret resides.

An ugly creature, alongside seven small, fluffy companions, each endowed with the ability to change colour according to their emotions. From anger, they turn blue; from sadness, yellow; and from happiness, pink. They are kept hidden by a king who fears their secret knowledge of how emotions shape reality through manifestation. Among them, the ugly creature possesses a unique gift – the ability to communicate with spirits and manipulate others with mere words.

From one perspective, keeping such power hidden is a blessing, as its unleashed potential could lead to chaos.

Yet, the ugly creature believes it is best kept secret, using its abilities discreetly. Locked away in a basement, these creatures require neither food nor sustenance, existing eternally. However, secrets seldom remain hidden forever. One day, a young girl who stumbled into this world by accident gets lost in this very forest. As she wanders and inspects her way out of the luscious green of the forest, she meets the magical beings. Unaware of the danger that lurks, she is drawn to the friendly demeanour of the fluffy creatures, who transform into shades of pink, filling her with joy.

Enthralled by the girl's innocence, the ugly creature mimics her, unleashing a cascade of unforeseen events. The girl, captivated by the enchantment, becomes ensnared in the magic of the creatures, unaware of their true power.

In her blissful ignorance, she meets her end, an inevitable death, surrounded by the outlandish creatures and their bizarre colours.

In another world of her imagination, Ramy sees a castle with green colours in combination with purple and dark blue, sound waves that can be seen.

In our world, this does not exist.

However, in this world, music is seen as water making waves in the ocean, sound waves that surround the castle and create a place of charm in Ramy's mind.

In this castle, she sees a fairy who is carrying a heavy pot with stones, but she can't carry it by herself. So, another dwarf helps her. "Why are you carrying those? They are just stones!" he exclaims. "Please help me; they are not just stones; they are gold if we can carry them through that tunnel.

Can you help me, please?" The dwarf helps the fairy but at the same time scolds her in a language that only he knows, thinking it impossible.

Both of them carry that pot of stones up a spiral of stairs that leads to the tunnel. There, they find a door aged for thousands of years that has not been opened for a very long time. Struggling to open the door, they finally succeed. After closing the door, everything turns into gold. The dwarf is amazed at what he sees, captivated by so much gold that surrounds the tunnel. The fairy laughs and thanks the dwarf for his help.

In another dimension, Ramy finds herself in a world of unicorns. They look at each other and move across, having a telepathic conversation. Ramy sees those unicorns, and they bow in front of her as if she owns their kingdom.

She walks in light towards a skyscraper, bends down in front of them, and with just a look, she makes herself understood. No words, no sound, nothing; she conveys thanks and gratitude in thought.

In another world of her imagination, Ramy is protected by a dragon. She stands in front of a cursed door that, once touched, steals five years of one's life, making them grow old. The door appears ordinary, but the dragon warns Ramy that a spirit, killed by Evil, is trapped inside. The spirit's last moments were captured by the door, and with her dying breath, she cursed anyone who touches it to lose years of their life.

The dragon, who accompanies Ramy through the walls of an old building, shares many secrets hidden within those walls. The dragon tells her that she is an innocent soul, protected from above. However, the dragon also warns her that Evil is upon her, threatening her. "I will be here for you whenever you need me," the dragon reassures her.

And Ramy wakes up, scared.

Ramy's favourite season is winter, so her emotions are in tune with her desires and visions. One of her favourite visions is a quiet forest where the fir trees are covered by snow.

Snow falls quietly as she walks, and in the middle of the forest, she finds an old cottage. Inside, it is warm and cosy. She finds a beautiful Christmas tree with ornaments everywhere. It's Christmas time, and she discovers old books and a hot chocolate waiting for her. Wondering who made all of this, she falls asleep. When she wakes up, she meets a guy who seems to know her.

"Hi, Ramy!" he says.

Ramy is confused. "Who are you?"

I am no one," he replies with a slow and soothing voice.

Then, Ramy wakes up in the real world, feeling a little bit weird.

These portals of her imagination are like opening a movie in front of her, where the fiction comes alive and can be closed whenever she wants to. Over time, she learns to take control of her emotions and balance the fiction world with reality, helping her to take information from there and aiding herself in the real world. Releasing her emotions into the other world makes her more powerful each day.

***

One day as Ramy meditates, she loses herself in another world, a world that she had just been exploring since a while, for a few moments. There, she encounters an entity that guides her to a water well.

At first, she's afraid, but the friendly entity encourages her to descend. A ladder leads down into the well, and as she climbs, she smells something wet and fresh. Yet, it isn't water. The liquid touches her skin and emits a strange hissing sound, almost like gold being heated.

Inside the well, Ramy finds several numbered doors. The entity gestures for her to choose between doors numbered 3, 5, or 8. Strange symbols resembling hieroglyphs and an inverted triangle mark each door. Confused, she asks, "Why can't I go through all of them?"

"You can only choose one path, child. Time is running out. Choose now!" the entity urges.

With little time to decide, she picks door number 8. As she enters, a dark cloud looms, and a distant candlelight flickers in the far corner. The entity warns her: "Be careful. This room seems empty, but it is not. The darkness is deceptive, and the light is not what you think."

The entity's form fades in and out like a shadow as it adds, "You've chosen a difficult path, my girl!" It then laughs, its voice turning sinister. "You'll be lost here forever."

Hypnotized by the faint light, Ramy moves toward it, step by step.

She reaches the candle, only to find it leads to another room with yet another distant light.

She feels trapped, and when she tries to turn back, there is no door, no entity—only emptiness.

Suddenly, a black hole appears around her. She steps into it, overwhelmed with fear, and begins to cry. Then, a calming voice pulls her toward the light outside, and she finds herself surrounded by clouds of emotions. As she walks, she encounters drops of happiness, fear, anger, and calmness, each step bringing her through a different emotion.

Eventually, she arrives on a larger cloud and falls asleep. When she wakes, it's back to reality, with a headache and a faint laugh on her lips.

In another meditation, Ramy shifts the frequency of the music, finding herself in a world of crystals. Each crystal holds hidden information from civilizations that existed long before humans. Inside an underground cave, the crystals are vibrant, each glowing with a different color. As she touches them, a sense of calm washes over her, and she connects with their energy, seeing creatures from other realms—beings vastly different from humans.

She walks among the crystals, and a portal opens before her. Ramy decides not to enter, choosing instead to stay in the cave with the magical crystals.

They contain knowledge beyond her imagination, pulling her mind into realms far from normality. She feels chosen, a guardian of secrets, aware that others would dismiss her experiences as mere dreams.

One day, Ramy taps into a different frequency of sound and enters a timeless spiral, a place beyond space. Here, she sees futures and parallel worlds opening like a book. In every version of herself, she is different—each incarnation leading to a unique path of evolution. It's as though she's standing in a library of time, watching her ancestors, her parents, and the people she works with, all fighting to evolve, to spiritually ascend faster, to avoid the cycle of reincarnation.

It amuses Ramy, this struggle over time, when time itself doesn't exist. She laughs, realizing how limited human perception is in the physical world. Time is merely a construct of the mind, but in the spiritual realms, everything operates on a different frequency. Ramy enjoys the peace of this place, wanting to stay there forever. But she is suddenly pulled back into her body, waking up with vivid memories. She wonders if it was all a dream, but the clarity of the experience tells her otherwise.

That place—the library of time— fascinates her, as it felt like the most beautiful dream she had ever experienced. She saw spirals of time, so much information about the people she knew.

Each soul had a purpose. Going back to Earth after such a monumental experience made everything seem trivial. Life felt like a game, one where you never know if you'll win or what awaits at the next level.

In this journey, Ramy realizes that Planet Earth is an illusion—real, yet not real. Life, as humans know it, is merely a chapter in the spirit's journey, one that vanishes after death. Money, power, material things—they all disappear. As you age, you can no longer enjoy them. And in one sudden moment, everything can change. No wealth or power can stop aging, illness, or death. This world, she understands, is only a vacation for the spirit, a place to learn lessons.

The information given to Ramy in her dream makes her realize that the world she once fought for is merely an illusion. Dying is not something to fear, but rather a return home—a place of freedom. For Ramy, it's a profound understanding. Though life may feel like a curse, death is a blessing. Yet, she remains bound to this 3D world, even if she doesn't want to be.

This other world brought Ramy to life, immersing her in magic and wonder, free from the troubles of reality. It was a place where she could forget her problems and lose herself in enchantment.

But, inevitably, reality always found a way to wake her up.

Conflict

Conflict

Ramy was diving deeper into the spiritual world, and it was changing her. She was drifting away from normal life, and Michael couldn't bring her back. She was more and more absorbed by her visions and the magic of other dimensions, losing touch with the real world.

But one day, the reality in her irony woke her up with an unpredictable change that was coming her way.

Michael got very sick, and she was worried about his health, so they decided to go for a consultation; after a while, he recovered, and even though the doctors said he was fine, Ramy felt something was wrong. With her newfound intuition which she was beginning to trust, she persuaded Michael to go back to the hospital for more tests.

Indeed, the inner voice that urged Ramy to force Michael to take this seriously turned out to be telling the truth as he discovered he had a serious illness and didn't have much time left, but Michael chose not to tell Ramy.

As the illness took its toll, Michael tried to protect Ramy by pushing her away.

One evening, he forced himself to have a tough conversation with her.

"Ramy," he said, his voice filled with sorrow, "I think it's better if you leave me. You have your whole life ahead of you. You're young, beautiful, and smart..." His voice faltered, but he looked right into Ramy's eyes, and uttered the words that would taint her soul for a lifetime. "I need you to leave me. I want to leave you."

Ramy was shocked. "No, Michael. I can't imagine my life without you. This is crazy," she replied, refusing to accept his words.

Unable to tell her the truth, Michael started behaving strangely.

He would disappear at night, going to clubs and parties, even seeing other women. He hoped this would make Ramy leave, but he couldn't bring himself to end things completely. Their relationship became a mess of arguments and mixed signals.

Ramy didn't know about Michael's illness and was confused by his behavior.

Their once stable relationship turned into a constant struggle. The stress made Ramy sick too, but Michael seemed not to care.

One evening, after another argument about his behavior, Michael locked himself in the bathroom, staring at the mirror.

He could not recognise the man he had become. His body was failing him, but worse than that was the guilt festering in his soul.

"If only I could make her leave," he muttered, knowing he couldn't bear to drag her through his suffering. But instead of talking to her, he let the frustration manifest in reckless decisions—staying out late, drinking, and surrounding himself with fleeting distractions that did nothing but deepen the void in his life.

Ramy, on the other hand, was drifting between the physical and spiritual worlds.

As Michael became more distant and erratic, her spiritual practices intensified.

Her dreams became vivid journeys into another dimension where she found solace, clarity, and, above all, peace. In these dreams, she encountered a figure—a mysterious presence who embodied the love, calm, and understanding that Michael no longer could give her. Each time she woke up from these visions, a part of her felt relieved, as if this alternate reality was offering her a future without pain.

As the days wore on, Ramy could no longer recognize the man she had spent the last decade with.

His cruelty shocked her—the late-night disappearances, the coldness, the aggression. She found herself questioning every memory, every moment they had shared. Was this the real Michael, or had he been hiding this side of himself all along?

Yet, even as she questioned him, Ramy couldn't stop trying to understand. She tried to look past the hurt, the betrayal, and the sudden shift in their relationship. With every tear shed in frustration, she turned to her spiritual guides for answers. They showed her visions of Michael's inner turmoil, and though her heart ached for him, she began to let go.

The more she saw his destructive behavior, the more her emotions dulled, like a fire slowly burning out.

One day, when Michael came home after another night out, smelling of alcohol and cheap cologne, Ramy finally confronted him. "Who are you, Michael?" she asked, her voice barely above a whisper.

"I don't know you anymore." The declaration was filled with pain.

He stared at her with cold eyes, the love they once shared buried under layers of pain and anger. "You're right," he replied flatly. "Maybe you never did."

The words stung, but deep down, Ramy knew she was losing him not because of another woman or his cruel actions, but because something much darker was at play. She just didn't know how deep the darkness ran.

As Michael's condition worsened, so did his behavior.

He became reckless at work, nearly losing his job. He threatened to hurt her if she left but also begged her to stay away from him. But, when Ramy tried to leave, Michael threatened to kill himself.

It was then that she realized how trapped they both were—him by his illness and pride, her by her love and guilt.

Ramy's spirit guides continued to visit her in dreams, urging her to look beyond the material world. The love she encountered in the other realm began to heal her.

Slowly, she stopped feeling any guilt for Michael's suffering. She couldn't save him, and she couldn't save herself if she stayed.

In her dreams, a figure reminded her that her path was meant to be different – that Michael was no longer the man she was destined to be with.

Michael, on the other hand, was consumed by his illness. The pain and fear twisted him into a version of himself he barely recognized. He wanted to push Ramy away to protect her, but instead, his cruelty only bound them closer in a toxic dance of suffering. He resented himself for it but couldn't stop. He couldn't let her go, and he couldn't hold on.

Their decision to stay friends, at least on the surface, was a last-ditch effort to maintain some semblance of control.

Ramy hoped therapy would help Michael, but he tricked the therapists,

pretending everything was fine, all while his body and soul decayed.

Meanwhile, Ramy's spiritual awakening reached new heights. She astral projected frequently, leaving behind the chaos of her waking life to explore realms where love, light, and peace awaited her. She no longer needed Michael for emotional support; she found it within herself and the universe.

By the time she was ready to walk away for good, Ramy had transformed. She was no longer the fragile soul Michael had once known. She had become something else—stronger, wiser, and unbound by the constraints of earthly love.

The Lover

The Lover

One day, while the echoes of Michaels' sneering voice from the latest argument were still ringing in Ramy's ears as she retreated to her room, she felt a sudden doom was making its way towards her. The conflict with Michael had left her feeling drained and disheartened. He couldn't understand the changes she was undergoing, the deep transformation reshaping her very being.

She couldn't understand why he couldn't show a single bit of kindness towards her while she was doing her best to cater to the changes that had taken place in their relationship.

Their marriage, once a source of stability, had become a battlefield of misunderstandings and unmet expectations.

As she prepared for her nightly meditation, Ramy felt the familiar pull of the astral realm, the place where she would go in her dreams or when music fell in her ears, beckoning her to a place where she found solace and connection.

Ramy closed her eyes and felt her consciousness detach from her physical body. She was in the astral realm again, a place where time didn't matter and her deepest emotions found expression. It was here, in this ethereal space, that she first met him—the man who would change her life forever. He was only a silhouette, devoid of flesh, but so beautiful.

At first, Ramy didn't recognize the significance of their encounter. She wandered through a landscape that felt both strange and familiar, her soul guided by an unspoken longing.

The air shimmered with an otherworldly light as she moved, her footsteps silent on the soft, glowing ground. Suddenly, she felt a presence beside her. Turning, she saw him: a figure bathed in a gentle, golden glow, his eyes filled with warmth.

"Ramy," he said, his voice like a melody she had always known but forgotten. Could it be this melody that had something to do with her soulful connection with music?

"Who are you?" she asked, though a part of her already knew the answer.

"I will show you who I am. Close your eyes and now breathe..."He approached her kindly.

As he spoke, visions flooded Ramy's mind—fragments of their shared past, lifetimes spent together in joy and sorrow. She saw their first meeting, ages ago, when they were both new to this world. They had pledged their love to each other then, sealing their fates with an energetic cord that linked their souls across time and space.

Through countless lives, they had found each other again and again, their connection unbroken even in death.

Ramy felt a profound sense of recognition and relief.

She had always felt different, as if a part of her was missing. Now she understood why. The emotions that had always seemed too intense, the visions that had puzzled her— these were all echoes of her love for him, a love that transcended lifetimes.

In the astral realm, there was no need for words. Their souls communicated directly, sharing thoughts and feelings with a clarity that was impossible in the physical world.

He could see all her struggles, her fears, and her hopes. She was him, and he was all of her and more. They were like lost pieces of each other's souls.

This connection gave Ramy a feeling of strength like she had never felt before. She began to understand her inner power, the true extent of her abilities.

Her journeys into the astral realm became more frequent, and each time she met him, she returned to the physical world with a clearer mind and a stronger heart. She was no longer the emotional, uncertain girl she once was.

She had become logical, powerful, and self-possessed.

In these higher planes, Ramy met her true love—a soul connection far deeper than anything she'd ever experienced with Michael.

She understood now that Michael was part of her journey, but he wasn't meant to stay. The support she received from the other world gave her the strength to finally detach from Michael, even though he remained lost in his own suffering.

Back in the real world, Michael was a man in turmoil. He watched helplessly as Ramy drifted further from him, her presence a ghostly shadow of the woman he once knew. There was surely guilt, as he knew he was the reason why she had flown way apart, but he still wanted her to fight.

Because that is what she was all about.

That is what he had seen her doing all her life – Fighting.

Michael was unaware of what she had finally found amidst all the heartache and pain that she had been forced to face ever since she had become an existence in this broken world. The immediate consequence of this, though, was the deafening silence in their home.

Michael couldn't fathom the depth of Ramy's transformation, nor could he understand the invisible force that seemed to pull her away from him. He loved her deeply, but that love was now tinged with confusion and fear. His attempts to reach her, to rekindle the connection they once shared,

were met with an emotional wall he could not breach.

Ramy's transformation did not go unnoticed. Those around her saw the change but could not understand its source. Earthly love no longer held any allure for her. She had experienced a love so deep, so eternal, that no mortal relationship could compare. Her heart was locked, the key held by her lover in the astral realm.

Her intuition warned her of the coming troubles, but the pull of the spiritual world was too strong.

Ramy balanced between two worlds, seeking comfort in her dreams while facing the tragic reality of her life.

The road ahead was tough, but Ramy was determined to face it with the strength she had gained from her spiritual awakening.

The Ultimate Trial

The Ultimate Trial

In this world, Ramy and Michael's relationship had now devolved into a never-ending series of arguments. The ancient love that had once bound them was replaced with resentment and mistrust.

Michael sought escape in the nightlife, frequenting clubs and parties, even turning to prostitution as their life spiralled further into chaos.

The breaking point came when Michael, unable to tolerate their fractured relationship any longer, gave Ramy one month's notice to leave the house. The timing could not have been worse. Ramy had just lost her job and faced an uncertain future.

On a gloomy and unusually dark night, as Ramy sat by the window thinking about what in the world she was supposed to do, she felt a fierce orange glow behind her.

When she turned her heard, in her horror, she saw that the candle fire had caught a piece of the curtain, and it was engulfed in angry, raging fire.

The first emotion that hit her was shock. She looked around in complete hysteria, her eyes looking for an exit, but the front door was a big ball of smoke and flames. Then fear kicked in, and she ran towards the other window and tried to open it, but the knob refused to move an inch. Her body, trembling at this point, was now shutting down with the amount of cortisol pumping in her veins. Soon, blackness started to gather in front of her.

Her eyes threatened to close, her brain losing consciousness. The last thing she heard was a thud. It was her own body falling on the floor.

When she opened her eyes, she found herself in all the worlds she had been seeing for so long. There, she met her lover, the dragon, and all the beings from the Unseen World who had been invisible to her in her world but now seemed so real.

Her lover welcomed her with open arms, excited to have her with him for an endless time. But to his surprise, the truth was far from this dream of his.

The Lorzi of Karma, the Gods, decided to send her back to Earth. They talked and whispered many secrets among themselves, and Ramy along with the Lover waited and waited the outcome.

The Lorzi of Karma and the Unseen World knew that her journey in her world was not to end yet. They decided to erase her memories of these worlds and experiences, after she is sent back to her world.

"Please, let her stay..." The Lover pleaded.

"Boy, she is not ready. She is to go back to her world, and find her own reasoning. Her time is not yet to be over." The Lorzi of Karma stated.

"Pleas—" The Lover wanted to beg at this point.

"Stop! You are not to make any contact with her now when she returns. You are only

to be united once the death is ready to take her life in her world. Ready without an intervention!" The Gods commanded.

The Lover understood one thing with a deep hurt in his heart – the only thing he could do was watch her from the Astral plane and wait for her to die so they could finally be together for eternity, never returning to Earth. He had to wait patiently for her to die. His love for her was worth thousands of millennia, so what would a few decades of wait matter for him?

The Lorzi of Karma had their own reasons as well.

They wanted to send Ramy back because she still had karma to complete before she could finally be free and not return to Earth again.

Ramy was witnessing the exchange of words and emotions among the Gods and her Lover, but there wasn't anything that her mind was able to register. A sudden ache, starting from head, took charge and reached her heart. It hit her body like a bolt of thunder, and she collapsed, once again.

Ramy opened her eyes to a reality that was completely erased from her mind. She forgot everything upon her return to Earth.

***

As days turned into weeks and weeks into months, Michael's life took a dramatic turn. A series of troubling incidents at work led to a psychiatric evaluation, where he was diagnosed with borderline personality disorder. Instead of seeking help, Michael threw himself deeper into a hedonistic lifestyle, indulging in parties, women, drugs, and alcohol. His regret over losing Ramy gnawed at him, but he was unable to turn back the clock.

As the months passed, Michael's reckless lifestyle caught up with him.

His body, worn out by substance abuse, finally gave in. He died peacefully, though his life had been anything but peaceful.

Even though Michael's story had reached its conclusion, Ramy's was only starting to begin.

The Descend

The Descend

The descend of Ramy back to her world came with lots of questions, moments of confusions, and a longing; an urge to reach out for something that she had lost, but she couldn't point her finger to what it was.

However, her life continued to move from one night to another. Angels were sent her way to bring her people, opportunities, and the right places to start her life again.

With no memory of what she had been all her life, it seemed difficult for her to find her way around others, but the most challenging was when she had to face her own self in loneliness.

Whenever she had a moment to herself after a long day of finding work, answers, and re-connecting with people who had been part of her life before, she would feel music creeping into her ears – it would come to her like a soothing balm on a long-forgotten wound.

The melody would instantly cause a wave of stillness in her body, and she would find herself closing her eyes, not having the strength to resist the sombreness of It all. That was the only way she was able to sleep.

Ramy had no recollection of her ascend to the other world, her meeting with her soul lover, and the way she was denied union with him by the Gods. This was done as a favour by the Lorzi of Karma, so she could fulfil what her destiny had in store for her – to finally satiate the wish of Karma. She could only do it without the pain of remembrance, it was too much for even her, an evolved spirit not meant for the world she had been born into.

However, there was another revelation that had taken place in the other world, unbeknownst to Ramy. It was that she did not have a single cell in her body that was offered any special power by the Gods or any other mystical element that made up her world. It was, after all, her lover who had been the cause of it all.

Apart from Ramy's unfulfilled Karma, the Lorzi of Karma were also concerned about the power that the couple would give birth to if they were to be together in the same world. Hence, they delayed their union.

Since Ramy's beginning in her world, she was watched over by him. Anything and everything that gave her a semblance of power was bestowed upon her by him, as it was his responsible to protect her. To bring her back to him in the other world, so they can live the rest of whatever the Gods will offer them with all the love they had stored just for each other.

The music, however, was a constant way to connect himself with Ramy in the life before the fire happened and after too.

As whenever a beat of music reached Ramy, her mind would flash with faded and blurred memories, a huge orange fire, a soft voice, crows in a group, and a blood-curdling scream, a shriek that she didn't know belonged to herself as she was falling away from the arms of the man who was truly meant to love her in the way she deserved.

Doctors had no answer to her queries, and most of them disregarded her symptoms, often giving one justification, which was memory loss due to an extremely traumatic experience, and that was all they could do for her.

Her lover spent his days and nights surveilling every movement of Ramy, awaiting her arrival. He kept the Lords' promise in high regard though – he knew in his heart that death would bring them together one day, but it hurt him to see that the new Ramy, the one who went back to her world after the descend, did not remember a thing; their soul-connection, their meetings, the way they could feel each other, even when they were thousands of light years apart.

In another world, Ramy's life was like a blank canvas, and she was painting it with hues, one day after another.

She was unaware of what fate had laid for her in her coming days, and it was only time that had the power to uncover the inevitable.

***

Ramy wasn't born special.

The Lover Spirit granted her all the abilities from the Other World to connect with him. However, since he is no longer allowed to do so, she is now just a normal woman. The only remnants of her past connection are the sounds of the music, which sometimes evoke a fleeting sense of the extraordinary.

Premonitions

Premonitions

In this chapter, I, the author, would like to have a personal conversation with you, my beloved reader, about premonitions.

Everyone has premonitions—those gut feelings about what will happen next in their life. From my experience, that feeling lingers when you are not on the right path. It's a gut feeling that resides in your heart no matter what, and I didn't dare to listen to it because I thought it was wrong. I believed I had to listen to my mind, not my emotional, fragile side.

Being controlled by emotions can be frightening. It took me a long time to balance my mind, feelings and intuition.

I always feel that a few days before someone passes away, I receive channelled messages from the unseen. I don't like to call it Spirit like everyone else; for me, it's the UNSEEN, and the messages are very clear.

At first, I thought they were just silly thoughts, but then they started to be repetitive, occurring too many times to dismiss.

At one point, they got too loud for me to ignore or brush them under the carpet.

I realized they were not silly at all and that I could use these premonitions to my advantage, not against me. If something bad approaches, I will know long before, especially concerning the people I love. Sometimes, I can warn them, and if they listen, they might avoid it. If it is written to happen, it will happen anyway, but "They" prepare me in advance, whether I can avoid the event or not, even the loss of someone.

Everyone can access these "premonitions" depending on their spiritual advancement and openness.

People who exist in the 3rd dimension live ordinary lives without feeling anything special. Their lives are quite normal, with problems that aren't too significant.

However, when someone approaches the 4th dimension, the trouble begins. The unseen start contacting you because you are open and ready to overcome obstacles. As creatures on this planet, we need to evolve no matter what.

The "you" of yesterday is not the "you" of today. If you went back in time, you would make different choices because you are different now from the "you from the future."

In the 5th dimension, a rare few on this planet can manifest everything they want and become Master Manifestors. All your wishes come true, but you can also quickly manifest all your fears.

Everything is in your mind, and if not controlled, your energy becomes more dense and clear, making it easier for evil to see and attack you.

With your evolution, your problems grow because you have the tools to overcome them.

Everything is already written;

I don't believe in free will, but that is just my personal opinion. In the 5th dimension, everything is possible with no limitations except those imposed by your mind.

Premonitions are a way for your spirit guides to warn you. If you are receptive enough, they can be a huge help or a curse.

Spiritual Conclusions

Spiritual Conclusions

In this chapter, I will share the lessons we can learn from the experiences of the main character, Ramy.

Ramy is not a victim of abuse; she is a survivor. Over time, she has grown stronger, overcoming her challenges with the help of the unseen.

In this story, there is a concept of destiny—no matter what you do, you will end up where you're meant to be.

Love can change over time, especially when your life is in danger. No matter how much you love someone, when they betray you and your life is at risk, there comes a point where you must choose to leave or stay. Continuing until self-care no longer exists only leads to a slow death from within.

One of the most important lessons I've learned is to forgive and accept that people are different. Over time, experiences change you into someone you never imagined you could be.

Time is a great teacher, and it has a lesson in every dip and high of life for you. It holds a mirror for you at every turn so you can see yourself where you are going.

Nobody truly knows you—not even those who've spent years with you, not even your parents. Only you have access to your full potential and to who you really are.

The universe—or God—gives you all the tools to overcome life's obstacles. Even when you think there's no way out, someone or something will come to help. This is why it's so important to have faith and believe in yourself.

Dreams are more than just dreams; we are traveling in the astral plane. From there, we gather the information we need. Some people can even access glimpses of their future.

We have multiple potential futures, but a few key points are set at the beginning of our journey on this planet.

Our souls choose the lives we will live before we are born. We have soul contracts that must be fulfilled before we die. If not, we may continue in another lifetime to accomplish what we agreed to from the start.

We decide our path—no one else chooses for us.

This planet is a school. We didn't come here to be happy; we came here to overcome challenges and clear the debts from our past lives. There's so much more beyond what we can see with our physical eyes—things that go beyond our imagination.

Even people who seem bad, like Michaela, play a role. Michaela's presence forces Ramy to become stronger, preparing her for the next level of darkness. When you encounter someone who seems bad, remember that you may meet someone even worse until you learn to stand up for yourself or choose a different path.

When trauma occurs in your life, try to see it as an opportunity to learn, rather than judge it. Look at yourself from outside the experience, not from within. It may be difficult at first, but with time, everything will make sense.

It's easy for us to judge one another, but hard to truly understand each other.

We humans have three major fears: the fear of loneliness, the fear of disease that renders us powerless, and the fear of death. Inevitably, we will face at least one of these, yet we are often taught to avoid confronting our fears. Instead, we bury them, thinking they will happen in a faraway future or pretend they won't happen. When they do come, many people lose themselves. How we handle these fears depends on our mindset and personality.

Everyone's love language is different. Each of us sees love from a unique perspective. In reality, love can be the greatest trap in the matrix. Many of us mistake love for deep attachment.

When we die, it becomes difficult for the soul to cut ties with loved ones because of these attachments. The inability to let go can destroy a person, making it hard to move on.

We must remember that we are born alone, and we die alone. No one can stay with us forever—not in this dimension. Some people even commit suicide due to the pain of losing loved ones. These individuals should not be judged or condemned. Their burden was too heavy to bear. After death, they realize it was only an illusion, but by then it's too late. They must reincarnate again and again.

I don't believe they go to hell—there's no hell, only lower dimensions where they may be trapped for a while. However, that's just my opinion; everyone has their own belief system.

In my perspective, sometimes real love is the strength to leave the other person to go on without you, even if that destroys you inside. Just to know that it is okay for them to be with someone else if it is not possible to be with you. This is a strength that not many of us can understand or can do in reality.

The truth is the world we live in is full of paradoxes.

While one person struggles just to survive, another can have everything they want. While some love deeply, like empaths, others care little, like narcissists. You never know who is standing before you—everyone has many layers.

We live in a hidden world, full of illusions, lies, and masks.

Throughout my life, I've tried to be a good person. But that doesn't necessarily mean I am one. I've faced dark times, yet somehow, I overcame every obstacle. I found myself in the darkness, where I had lost myself long ago.

I don't blame anyone for anything. Now I understand that there are no "good" or "bad" experiences—there is no light without darkness, and no darkness without light.

Thank you for choosing to read my story. My purpose is to bring light and hope to those who are experiencing the dark night of the soul.

May God bless you!